For Linda

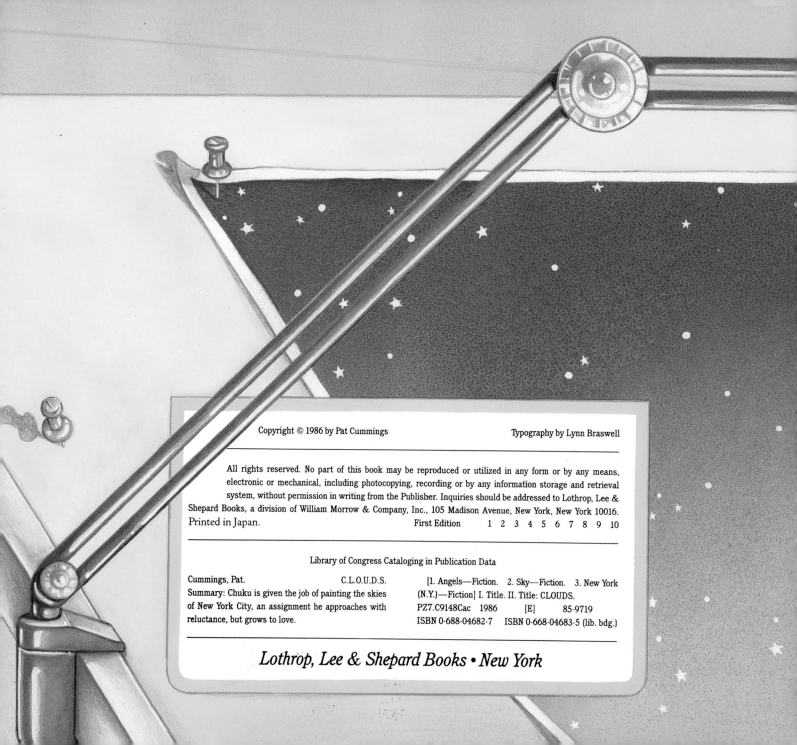

Library of Congress Cataloging in Publication Data

Cummings, Pat.   C.L.O.U.D.S.
Summary: Chuku is given the job of painting the skies
of New York City, an assignment he approaches with
reluctance, but grows to love.

[1. Angels—Fiction.   2. Sky—Fiction.   3. New York
(N.Y.)—Fiction] I. Title. II. Title: CLOUDS.
PZ7.C9148Cac 1986   [E]   85-9719
ISBN 0-688-04682-7   ISBN 0-668-04683-5 (lib. bdg.)

Lothrop, Lee & Shepard Books • New York

C.L.O.U.D.S.

by PAT CUMMINGS

Chuku had just come to work at the department of Creative Lights, Opticals, and Unusual Designs in the Sky.

The supervisor had assigned someone to show him around. He had spent the morning learning where the gossamer and lightbeams were kept. He'd received a key to the Hue Room, where all the colors were stored.

And now he sat at his drawing table waiting for his assignment. Finally a messenger knocked on his door and, with a sarcastic "Congratulations," dropped off a large manual. Attached to the front was a memo.

CLOUDS

CREATIVE LIGHTS, OPTICALS, AND UNUSUAL DESIGNS IN THE SKY

From: The Supervisor
To: Chuku

Welcome to our department. As you will read in the manual, it is our policy to start junior artists in the less demanding areas. You'll be designing skies for the city of New York. I hope you will see this as the good training program it is. I'm confident that you'll be able to work your way up in no time at all. The manual should answer all your questions. Good luck!

He read the memo twice. New York did not sound like what he had hoped for: It sounded like a job no one else wanted. He quickly leafed through the pamphlet, occasionally reading the rules that were starred.

* Only those with two years of experience may use the special effects laboratory.

* Absolutely no words or numbers allowed!

* Please submit all sketches for Spectacular Sunsets no later than noon for approval. (Check section 7 for geographical limitations.)

And so on…

Chuku was anxious to get started. Consulting the maps in the back of the manual, he immediately left for the western sector to inspect the New York sky.

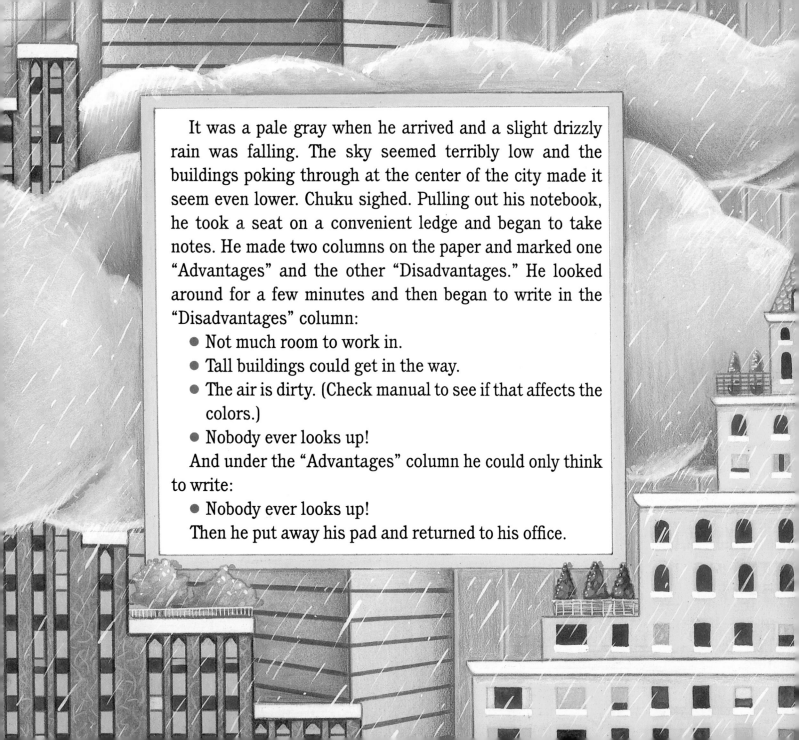

It was a pale gray when he arrived and a slight drizzly rain was falling. The sky seemed terribly low and the buildings poking through at the center of the city made it seem even lower. Chuku sighed. Pulling out his notebook, he took a seat on a convenient ledge and began to take notes. He made two columns on the paper and marked one "Advantages" and the other "Disadvantages." He looked around for a few minutes and then began to write in the "Disadvantages" column:

- Not much room to work in.
- Tall buildings could get in the way.
- The air is dirty. (Check manual to see if that affects the colors.)
- Nobody ever looks up!

And under the "Advantages" column he could only think to write:

- Nobody ever looks up!

Then he put away his pad and returned to his office.

Once at his table, he took out a large sheet of paper and sent to the Hue Room for a bottle of Classic Sunny-Day Blue. He spent the rest of the afternoon sketching a very plain blue sky that would cover the city the next day.

The supervisor called Chuku to his office before he left work to look at the sketch. "Lovely," said the supervisor.

"But it's just plain blue," said Chuku.

"Well, son," the supervisor answered, "you're just starting. Can't get too carried away. It'll be just fine." And he smiled a knowing smile as Chuku left.

The next morning the weathermen beamed on televisions and boomed over radios: "What a lovely day, not a cloud in the sky!" When Chuku heard that, he decided the supervisor must have known what he was talking about.

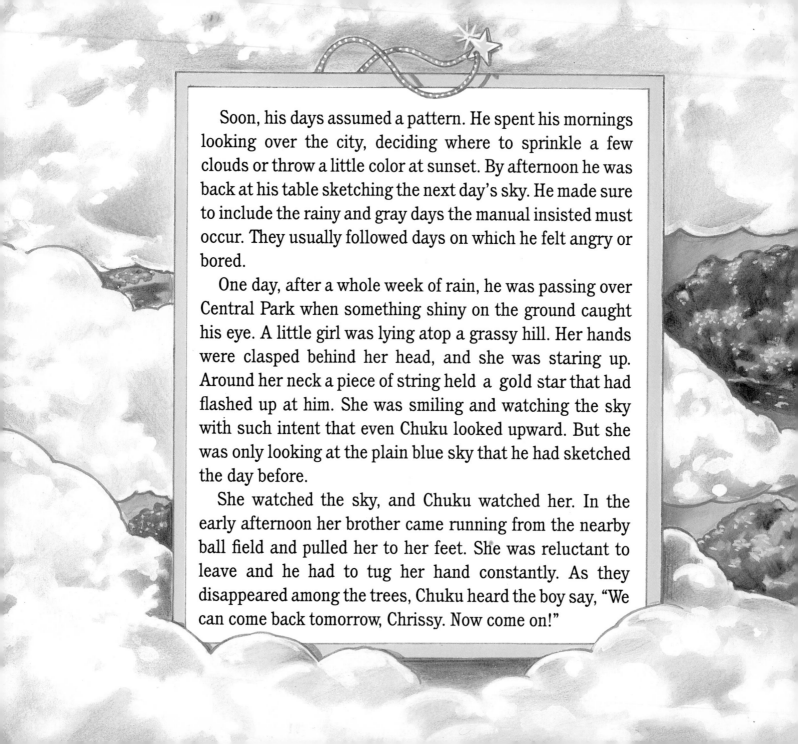

Soon, his days assumed a pattern. He spent his mornings looking over the city, deciding where to sprinkle a few clouds or throw a little color at sunset. By afternoon he was back at his table sketching the next day's sky. He made sure to include the rainy and gray days the manual insisted must occur. They usually followed days on which he felt angry or bored.

One day, after a whole week of rain, he was passing over Central Park when something shiny on the ground caught his eye. A little girl was lying atop a grassy hill. Her hands were clasped behind her head, and she was staring up. Around her neck a piece of string held a gold star that had flashed up at him. She was smiling and watching the sky with such intent that even Chuku looked upward. But she was only looking at the plain blue sky that he had sketched the day before.

She watched the sky, and Chuku watched her. In the early afternoon her brother came running from the nearby ball field and pulled her to her feet. She was reluctant to leave and he had to tug her hand constantly. As they disappeared among the trees, Chuku heard the boy say, "We can come back tomorrow, Chrissy. Now come on!"

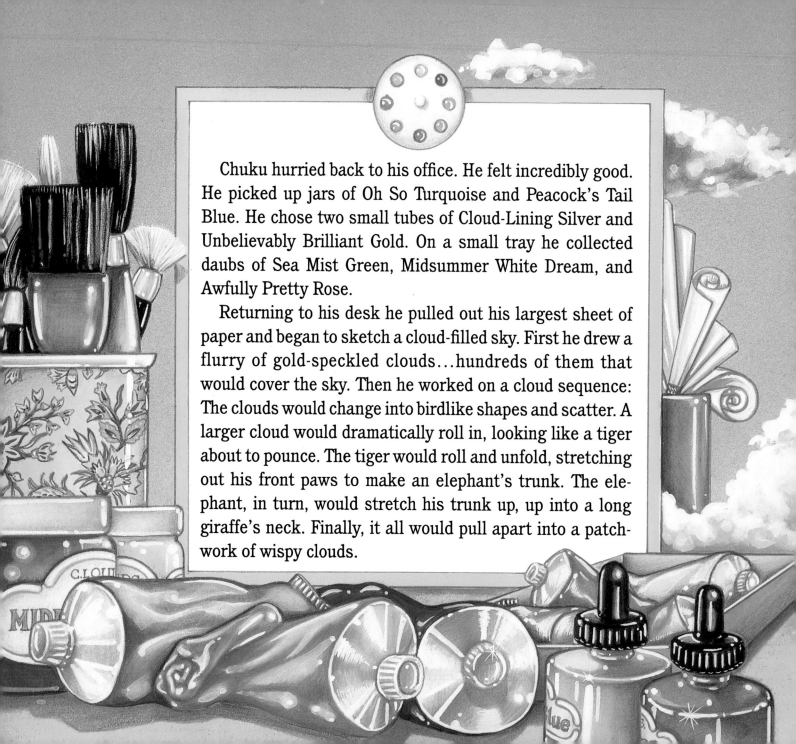

Chuku hurried back to his office. He felt incredibly good. He picked up jars of Oh So Turquoise and Peacock's Tail Blue. He chose two small tubes of Cloud-Lining Silver and Unbelievably Brilliant Gold. On a small tray he collected daubs of Sea Mist Green, Midsummer White Dream, and Awfully Pretty Rose.

Returning to his desk he pulled out his largest sheet of paper and began to sketch a cloud-filled sky. First he drew a flurry of gold-speckled clouds...hundreds of them that would cover the sky. Then he worked on a cloud sequence: The clouds would change into birdlike shapes and scatter. A larger cloud would dramatically roll in, looking like a tiger about to pounce. The tiger would roll and unfold, stretching out his front paws to make an elephant's trunk. The elephant, in turn, would stretch his trunk up, up into a long giraffe's neck. Finally, it all would pull apart into a patchwork of wispy clouds.

Chuku was exhausted. He had nine drawings before him. The entire thing would last a couple of hours, he figured. Then he'd end with a Lovely Light Lavender sunset, and throw in traces of the U.B. Gold and A.P. Rose.

When the supervisor saw the sketches, he raised his right eyebrow slightly, but said no more than his usual "Fine with me."

Then he stamped all nine designs with his special seal

APPROVED

and sent them down to the Production Department, as usual.

The next morning Chuku was back at the park, in an excellent spot for viewing both the sky and the little girl's reactions. She arrived shortly before the first tentative clouds rolled into place. Stretching out on the grass, she watched the bird shapes grow and fly off in all directions. As the tiger appeared, her mouth opened to a wide smile and only closed as the last shreds of giraffe stretched apart.

This time as her brother took her hand and led her home, her eyes remained glued to the quickly lavendering sky.

After they left, Chuku returned to his office. He felt terribly good again and immediately set to work.

Flowers sprouted from boats and snakes turned into ladders. He constructed castles that would dissolve into schools of fish at the slightest gust of wind. And with a well-placed breeze, he would send a swarm of butterflies into a huge outstretched hand.

Chrissy loved it. She was there every-day, except when it rained—and there were still rainy days. Chuku was careful to stick to the rules: He made sure that something was happening all over town, not just in the park. He found that the sky around tall buildings with reflecting glass windows was an excellent place to use bright colors. Over the rivers he often created his best rainbows and sunsets. He had truly begun to enjoy his job.

The supervisor had taken notice of this sudden burst of creativity, and eventually he sent word for Chuku to come to his office.

"You've been doing some lovely work, son," he said. "That's a particularly uninspiring area, but you've made advantages out of your disadvantages."

"Thank you, sir," Chuku replied modestly.

"In fact, the director himself has noticed. We've decided you're ready for a really nice location."

"B-but—" Chuku stammered.

"Don't thank me, son," the supervisor continued. "The director recognizes talent and told me personally that I could give you a tropical location. Now there's a winner! The colors they use in that area! You finish up the week in New York and next week I'll show you your new office."

Chuku was distressed. He knew it would be a mistake to refuse such a well-intentioned offer, but even the thought of leaving New York and Chrissy upset him.

"Thank you, sir," he said softly.

Chuku returned to his office. For a long time he sat at his desk staring at the paper he'd painted Ballet Slipper Blue. Then he picked up a piece of soft chalk and wrote across the center:

Hello down there.

He knew this would never be approved. The supervisor stuck to the rules strictly and words were absolutely forbidden. But he had to at least say something to Chrissy before he transferred to the tropics. So when the supervisor had left his office to inspect the new shipment of thunderbolts and rainbow parts, Chuku slipped in and used his rubber stamp.

The next afternoon he sat in the park watching Chrissy watch the sky for the last time. Slowly the words rolled into place. No airplane had written them and very few people even seemed aware of them. But Chrissy jumped to her feet and pointed at each word. She'd only recently been learning to read and her lips formed each word carefully as she read "Hello down there."

She began jumping and waving and jumping and smiling. Then the bird pattern he had used the first time he had drawn for her came drifting in. And as the birds flew apart in every direction, Chrissy's brother came and led her away. Just at the edge of the trees, she turned and waved again at the sky.

Chuku didn't feel like going back, so he wandered over the city taking his last look. He passed the Empire State Building where people were watching the sky through telescopes. He paused downtown at the Manhattan and Brooklyn Bridges and marveled at the reflections of his sky in the water. Everywhere people seemed to be looking up. In the World Trade Towers, executives stood at the windows dictating letters, and people on coffee breaks chatted and watched small clouds drift by. Uptown at the library park and in Columbus Circle, musicians were playing and couples leaned back on park benches, their dark glasses reflecting the sun. And up in Morningside Park, children of all sizes dotted the grass and pointed at his cloud formations. Chuku had never felt so good about his job and so bad about leaving. He remembered that only a short while ago, he had looked forward to being transferred.

Sadly, he returned to work only to find a memo pinned to his drawing table.

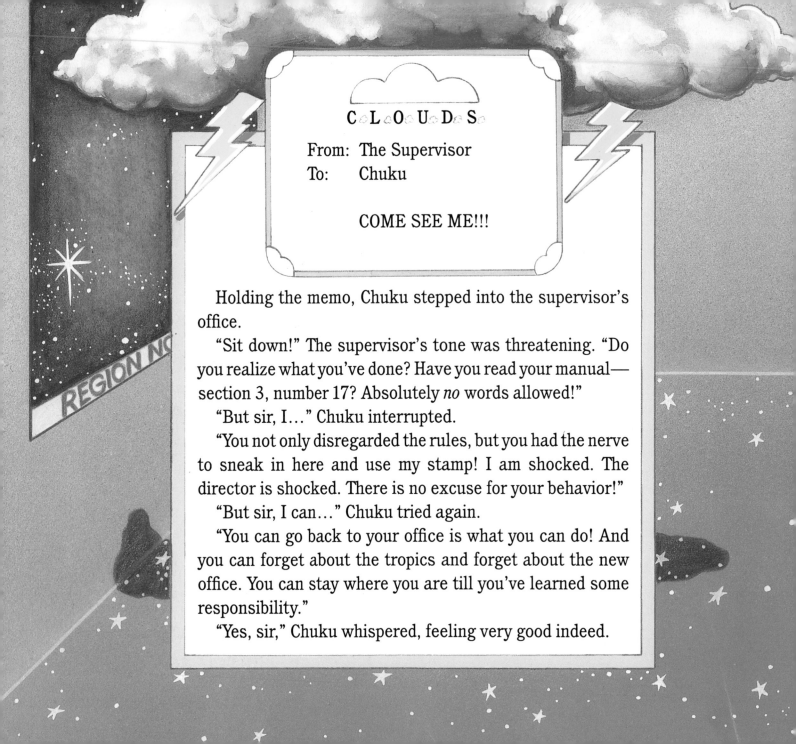

C L O U D S

From: The Supervisor
To: Chuku

COME SEE ME!!!

Holding the memo, Chuku stepped into the supervisor's office.

"Sit down!" The supervisor's tone was threatening. "Do you realize what you've done? Have you read your manual—section 3, number 17? Absolutely *no* words allowed!"

"But sir, I…" Chuku interrupted.

"You not only disregarded the rules, but you had the nerve to sneak in here and use my stamp! I am shocked. The director is shocked. There is no excuse for your behavior!"

"But sir, I can…" Chuku tried again.

"You can go back to your office is what you can do! And you can forget about the tropics and forget about the new office. You can stay where you are till you've learned some responsibility."

"Yes, sir," Chuku whispered, feeling very good indeed.

As he left the supervisor yelled after him "And you had better forget your sudden love for words, young man!"

Chuku smiled all the way back to his office. He felt so good that he hardly noticed all the disapproving frowns that peered at him through open doors marked MIDWEST and DOWN UNDER and FAR EAST.

He went in his office and painted a fancy sign to hang on his door. Then he sat down at his drawing table with a very contented look on his face and opened a new jar of Twilight Blue.